RUFF AN

Invasion of the ...

AGATHA

MAY YOUR TAIL
NEVER BE TANGLED!

RUFF AND TUMBLE

Invasion of the Dog Eating Yetis

First published by Books for Children 2013
© 2013 Royston Wood
ISBN: 978-0-9926960-1-6

The Moral right of the author has been asserted.

Contents

Chapter One

Scrabble®

Ruff stared hard at the letters on the rack in front of him. He was playing Making Words Out Of Letters Printed On Little Tiles By Putting Them On A Board, with Tumble. Tumble was winning.

But if I can just get one more word I'll win.

He scratched behind his ear with his back leg. This isn't as strange as it sounds because Ruff, or Rufus, is a dog; a shaggy, black, Scottish Terrier. He was hoping to rattle his Brain Cells into action.

Ruff has three Brain Cells. He uses two of them to do all the usual stuff,

like standing up, walking, eating and breathing. The third Brain Cell is saved for the really difficult things, like spelling.

The scratching didn't help. He still couldn't think of a word.

"Hurry up," snapped Thumbelina, or Tumble for short. And she is short: a stubby legged, brown and white Corgi, like the dogs the Queen of England has. She was sitting up very straight in her Day Bed, excited that she was about to win the game.

"Ok, ok! I'm thinking," mumbled Ruff, resting his shaggy black chin on the soft, cushioned edge of his Day Bed.

"I know, you've gone all cross-eyed," joked Tumble. "If you don't go soon you'll miss your turn and I'll win."

Ruff looked at his letters - SNOWNAM.

There must be a word I can get.

"Hurry up!"

Ruff Humphed loudly and scratched again.

"Times nearly up!"

Ah! I've got it. Brilliant!

"Times up!!"

Ruff shuffled his tiles onto the board – Ⓜ︎Ⓐ︎Ⓝ︎.

"Ha!" exclaimed Ruff. He added up his score, "That's one and one is two. And… ah…three more makes…er…lots."

Like all dogs, Ruff wasn't very good with numbers above three. Dogs tend to count like this, 'One, two, three, lots, lots and lots, lots and lots and lots'. Lots is a bit more than three, lots and lots is lots more than three and lots and lots and lots is lots and lots more than three.

9

"Soooo," gloated Ruff, "that means you have lots and lots and lots and I have lots and lots and lots *and* lots. So I win!! Ha!"

"Out of time!" snapped Tumble, leaping to her paws.

"No I wasn't!" growled Ruff, rising up on his own paws.

"YES YOU WERE!" barked Tumble leaning forward and scowling into Ruff's face.

"**NO I WASNT!**" snarled Ruff, pushing his nose up against Tumble's.

"CHEAT!"

"**LOOOOSERRR!!**"

Things could have turned NASTY but their argument was interrupted by the sound of

the Pack Leader's **NOISY METAL BOX THAT TRANSPORTS** arriving outside the Pack Lands. He had returned from the Daily Hunt. Ruff and Tumble stared at each other and then up at the kitchen clock. They had completely lost track of time.

Shoving the game board under the Big White Keep Things **COLD** Cupboard, they scurried over to sit by the kitchen door. They tried to make it look like they had been there all day, just waiting for the Pack Leader to come home.

There was the familiar **crunch** of gravel as the Pack Leader walked down the path. The key RATTLED in the front door and they heard it open and close again. Footsteps **THUDDED** across the lounge, into the dining room and then the kitchen door swung open.

"Hello doggies," said the Pack Leader, leaning down and tickling their ears. "Have you had a nice day?"

"Fine, fine. But we're in dire need of a Treat

from the Treat Cupboard," they responded.

Ruff and Tumble then started trying to make the Pack Leader give them a Treat.

Tumble went for a very straightforward approach. She walked over to the Treat Cupboard and glared at it, as if the power of her stare might **BURN** a hole in the door. She flicked the odd look at the Pack Leader, Beaming ferociously, "*Give the lovely doggie a treat, give the lovely doggie a treat*".

Ruff SKITTERED across the kitchen floor to the water bowl. He picked up his favourite toy, Rainbow Lion, from where he had dumped him in a puddle on the floor. Slinking past the Pack Leader into the dining room, Ruff dashed around the table **parping** Rainbow Lion by biting down on his middle. All the while he kept Beaming, "*Look at what I hunted today; perhaps I deserve a Treat.*"

Caught in a crossfire of double Beaming, the Pack Leader gave in. He opened the Treat Cupboard and pulled out one marrowbone Treat each.

Despite getting a Treat, Tumble gave a grunt of frustration. She was annoyed with herself for just standing there, **DRIBBLING**, thinking about the Treat, when she should have been watching closely to see exactly how the Treat Cupboard was opened.

Then I wouldn't have to keep Beaming at the Pack Leader for Treats. It's a lot of effort!

As she took the Treat from the Pack Leader's fingers she told herself that she would pay more attention next time. Then promptly forgot as she **crunched** her teeth in delight through the biscuit coating into the marrowbone middle.

Ruff was on guard duty with Rainbow Lion. They were perched on top of the back cushion of the 𝐛𝐢𝐠 𝐬𝐨𝐟𝐭 𝐜𝐨𝐦𝐟𝐲 𝐭𝐡𝐢𝐧𝐠, staring out of the window, ready to chase any INVADERS from the Pack Lands.

Rainbow Lion was helping Ruff with his job as Pack Protector. It was an important job. A few weeks ago Ruff had stopped an army of goblins from invading the Pack Lands.

Tumble helped occasionally. At least she did when things looked desperate. But most of the time she left it up to Ruff. Ruff found this strange because it was Tumble who had taught him the Pack Protector motto: Vigilance is Vital.

Ruff hadn't understood what that meant. So he had checked in his dictionary, which he used to look up tricky words in the books he read. The motto meant that it was really important to be alert and on the lookout for INVADERS all the time.

A loud SNORING from the cushions below interrupted his thoughts. Tumble was having Forty Winks after dinner.

Leaving all the pack protecting to me. Again.

Ruff stretched out one of his back legs and nudged Rainbow Lion, who leapt from the top of the back cushion straight onto Tumble's head. He **parped** loudly in her ear and then scurried quickly to the floor.

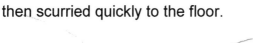

"Huh! Wha wuz tha..?" asked Tumble, waking from a deep sleep.

"What was what?" queried Ruff, still staring out of the window as if nothing had happened.

"Something landed on my head!" growled Tumble.

"Did it? I didn't see anything. And I should know because **I've** been looking out for things that might attack us, unlike you!" **grumbled** Ruff.

"It **parped** in my ear," mumbled Tumble. "And I was trying to have Forty Winks. I'm sure I didn't get more than lots!"

"Well, maybe if you were helping to protect the Pack Lands it wouldn't have sneaked in and woken you up. Whatever it was."

"Pah!" SNORTED Tumble, settling her head back on the sofa cushion. "I don't have to protect the Pack Lands."

Ruff frowned. "Vigilance is Vital! That's what you told me when I first arrived."

"Yes," agreed Tumble, closing her eyes and

settling deeper into the soft cushions. "It's very important."

Ruff's frown deepened to a scowl. "So why aren't you doing any **guarding** then?"

Tumble dragged an eyelid open and looked at Ruff through one eye. "$\mathcal{I}$ don't have to."

"What? Why?"

"Because one is a **Princess** and one has you to do one's jobs."

GRRRR!

Ruff growled and turned to stare out the window. *These conversations always end like this. Just because she's a stupid Corgi she thinks she's a lost* **Princess!** *All she does is*

lie around waiting for someone from the stupid Palace to turn up and whisk her away in a stupid golden carriage.

Tumble also said that Ruff was her servant, brought to the Pack Lands to look after her and do her bidding. *I don't mind doing some bidding (even if I'm not quite sure what it is) so long as it stops Tumble moaning at me all the time. But I'm not a servant!*

Humphing a little bit, Ruff rested his head on top of the big soft comfy thing and went back to being Vitally Vigilant.

Sometime later, he was startled awake. The Pack Leader had plonked himself heavily on the big soft comfy thing next to Tumble and switched on the Flickery Light Box With Noises. Ruff glanced about guiltily but fortunately nobody seemed to have noticed that he had been sleeping whilst on guard duty. Tumble was SNORING loudly and the Pack Leader was watching someone on the Flickery Light Box With Noises, who was sat behind a desk and droning on in a boring voice. He checked outside. Luckily the front garden wasn't full of Goblins or Trolls.

"And now over to Sally for the weather," the man on the Flickery Light Box With Noises was saying.

"Thanks Mike," a lady, most likely Sally, responded. "I hope you've got your hat and scarf ready because the big freeze is heading south! As we've just seen on the news, the snow has come to the north of the country unusually early, with temperatures reaching a record low for the time of year. Of course that hasn't stopped the kids enjoying the snow as we can see from these video clips sent in by our viewers..."

Ruff's ears pricked up at the mention of

snow. He was reading an excellent book at the moment; a spy thriller called 'Invasion of the Dog Eating Yetis'. It was about a load of Dog Eating Yetis, or abominable snowmen, trying to take over the fantasy realm by freezing the land and eating everyone. The story was full of snow but he had never seen any before and didn't really know what it was.

He had looked it up in his dictionary. snow; water vapour in the atmosphere that has frozen into ICE crystals and falls to the ground in the form of flakes. It hadn't helped much.

Scrambling to his paws, he wobbled round on the back cushion of the big soft comfy thing so he could look at the pictures on the Flickery Light Box With Noises. The ground in the video was all white and there were lots of people messing around in it. Some were throwing bits of white ground at each other, which was odd. Others were whizzing

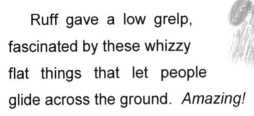

across the white ground stood on strange flat boards.

Ruff gave a low grelp, fascinated by these whizzy flat things that let people glide across the ground. *Amazing!*

But he still wasn't quite sure what 𝕤𝕟𝕠𝕨 was. *Is it white ground?*

In his book, the Dog Eating Yetis had sent 𝕤𝕟𝕠𝕨 to freeze the land before they invaded.

But this white ground doesn't seem to be troubling people. If anything they're whizzing around faster than normal on those flat whizzy things.

I wonder what they are? They're a bit like a surf board but for the white ground; the 𝕤𝕟𝕠𝕨. So what would you call that? Mmmm...maybe a snow surf board? But there isn't any surf.

Scratch Scratch

Maybe a snow glider?

That's whizzy.

A Whizzy Snow Glider!

Ruff carefully sneaked his notepad from his Back Pocket and flipped it open.

Not many people know that dogs have Back Pockets, but they do. They keep useful things in them, like spare Treats, mobile phones and notepads.

Ruff pulled out a stub of pencil and licked the end. Frowning and crossing his eyes in concentration, he wrote:

<u>Wish List</u>

1 x Whizzy Snow Glider

He was just carefully dotting his 'i's a scream from the Flickery Light Box With Noises made him look up. One of the people charging about on Whizzy Snow Gliders had just crashed and was buried head first in the snow.

Ruff licked the end of the pencil again and added to his list:

1 x helmet

He thought a bit and wrote:
...black...with a skull on it

He frowned and added:
(not an actual skull – just a picture)

Then he quickly stuffed the notepad into his Back Pocket before the Pack Leader could see what he was doing. Humans had certain ideas

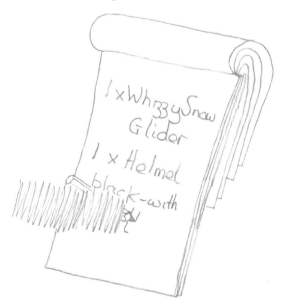

about dogs and it wouldn't do to change them.

If they ever find out how clever we really are they certainly won't let us lie around all day doing nothing.

Ruff settled down on the back cushion of the big soft comfy thing, his mind alive with images of snow and Whizzy Snow Gliders.

Chapter Two

Pickle My Toes

Ruff jerked awake. It took some time for his dream fogged mind to work out where he was. *I must be in my Night Bed.* He knew this because, firstly, he was curled up in something warm and soft. Secondly, Tumble's familiar, deep **rumbling** 𝕾𝕹𝕺𝕽𝕰 was coming from the bed next to his. And thirdly he could see the Big Bedroom door next to him, behind which the Pack Leader and Lead Female slept on the wonderfully soft Big Bed.

I don't remember coming to bed. The Pack Leader must have carried me upstairs.

He'd just been having an excellent dream.

I was escaping from lots of Dog Eating Yetis after stealing their secret plans. They were chasing me down a mountainside on Whizzy Snow Gliders. They almost had me! But then I tore down that narrow, zig zagging trail between those massive *snow* covered fir trees.

In his dream, Ruff had whipped between the fir trees, at a stupidly dangerous speed, and managed to lose the *Dog Eating Yetis*. He had just started grinning in delight when he had shot out over a cliff, high about a glittering lake.

It was the plunging through the air that had woken him up.

BRRRR!

He felt a bit shivery at the thought of falling, falling, falling...

I wish Tumble was awake.

Ruff hooked a paw over the edge of the fleecy mattress lining his Night Bed and pulled it back. Hidden underneath was a treasury of useful things: his book,
Invasion of the Dog Eating Yetis;
a dictionary; a large
chunk of bone,
in case he got
hungry;

his notepad, to jot down good ideas when they
came to him in the night; a lucky stone with a
hole in it; a Y shaped piece of stick that he was
keeping in the hope of find a piece of elastic, to
make a catapult; most of a bird's nest and
various other bits and pieces, including a
peacock feather that he had found at the zoo
and carried home in his Back Pocket.

Ruff grasped the pointy end of the feather in
his mouth. He slowly eased the fluffy end
towards Tumble's nose, which
wrinkled and
squirmed,
trying to

escape. But Ruff kept tickling until -

AAACHOOO!!

Ruff quickly shoved the feather back under his fleecy mattress and pretended to jerk awake.

"Hey, what! What's going on? Are we under attack?"

"Sorry," mumbled Tumble. "There was a feather tickling my nose. It made me sneeze."

Ruff frowned. "You woke me up to tell me that? Who's Heather anyway? And why would she want to pickle your toes to make cheese?"

"No, I said a feather was tickling my nose and it made me sneeze!"

Ruff lifted a paw and pointed it at Tumble, "Sounds like one of your stupid dreams to me. Fancy waking me up just to tell me about a stupid dream!"

"It wasn't a dream!" complained Tumble. "It felt real!"

"Of course," drawled Ruff, "because the place is just littered with feathers, floating

around to tickle your nose." As Ruff said this he noticed that, in lifting his paw to point it at Tumble, the tip of the peacock feather had sprung up. He quickly lowered his paw and squashed it back down.

"I'm sure it was real," mumbled Tumble, not sounding too sure.

"It was just a dream, Tumble. Now let's go back to sleep."

Ruff waited in silence until Tumble was just drifting back to sleep and then said, "Of course, if you did want to hear about a **really** real dream then I just had a brilliant one. It was epic!"

Tumble groaned. "Is this going to be like your last **really real** dream with all the goblins?"

"Hey! That wasn't just a dream. I saved the Pack Lands and *Righteous Rufus* saved the ꭙꩰꞥꞇꞏꞏꭙꭙ ꞧꞏꞏꞏꞏꞏꞏ at the same time."

"No. You dreamt you were Right Doofas, or

whatever his name was, because you were reading a book about him saving the 𝔉𝔞𝔫𝔱𝔞𝔰𝔶 𝔯𝔢𝔞𝔩𝔪 and then made up a whole story about goblins invading the Pack Lands to trick me."

"Rubbish!" snapped Ruff.

"Yes, it was: a whole load of made up rubbish."

"You know what I mean!" growled Ruff

"Ok. So what book are you reading at the moment?" asked Tumble.

Ruff grinned and rucked up his fleecy mattress with his paws until his book was spat out. The peacock feather also flew out and settled on the floor behind Ruff, just where he couldn't see it.

Tumble smiled.

Ruff must have woken me up with that feather to tell me about his dream. Maybe it will be the start of a new adventure. I quite enjoyed the last one. But I don't want Ruff to know that.

She replaced her smile with a scowl.

Ruff flicked through the pages of his book. "It's called, 'The Invasion of the Dog Eating Yetis' and it's all about an invasion of Dog Eating Yetis."

"You don't say?" drawled Tumble.

"I do say," said Ruff with a slight frown. He was puzzled because he had said and didn't understand that Tumble was being sarcastic.

"Now let me guess," said Tumble, "in your dream you were *Righteous Rufus*, Mighty Warrior and **Protector** of the 𝔉𝔞𝔫𝔱𝔞𝔰𝔶 𝔯𝔢𝔞𝔩𝔪, who had to defeat the Dog Eating Yetis."

"Ah," said Ruff, "that's where you've got it completely wrong! I wasn't *Righteous Rufus*, Mighty Warrior and **Protector** of the ƒ𝔞ℕ𝔱𝔞𝔰𝔶 ℝ𝔢𝔞𝔩𝔐, who had to defeat the Dog Eating Yetis.

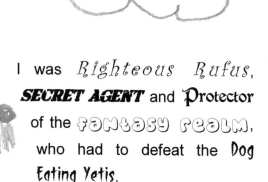

I was *Righteous Rufus*, **SECRET AGENT** and **Protector** of the ƒ𝔞ℕ𝔱𝔞𝔰𝔶 ℝ𝔢𝔞𝔩𝔐, who had to defeat the Dog Eating Yetis.

32

"Secret agent?" scoffed Tumble.

"No! **SECRET AGENT!** " corrected Ruff, shrinking his head into his shoulders, his eyes furtively darting looks left and right.

"Ok! **SECRET AGENT** then," mocked Tumble, mimicking Ruff.

"Yes! Working for the Government of the ℱ𝒶𝓃𝓉𝒶𝓈𝓎 𝓇𝑒𝒶𝓁𝓂 in their Mongrel Intelligence department – MI-lots."

"Well mongrel would suit you but I don't know about intelligence," said Tumble. "And the Government can't be all that bright either if it's recruiting the likes of you to be **SECRET AGENTS**."

"Well they have! So there! My codename's James Bone and I'm agent number **00-LOTS**, licensed to kill. So watch it!"

"Licensed to kill?" chuckled Tumble. "Licensed to heel more like!"

"Phaa!" said Ruff. "Take that back! You know I've never heeled in my life!"

Mmm. That's true, thought Tumble. *Scotties*

aren't very obedient. Not the best choice for a servant.

"Well, you're not much of a **SECRET AGENT** are you?" she mumbled.

"Why not!" demanded Ruff.

"Because you've only been one for five minutes and you've already told me your secret identity and code number."

"Oh yes," mumbled Ruff. "I suppose that wasn't being very secret."

Ruff slipped into a gloomy silence until a worrying thought dragged him out of it.

"You're not going to tell anybody are you?"

"I don't know. I might do."

"Oh please don't!" pleaded Ruff. "I'll be in all sorts of trouble if my secret identity gets out."

"So, what's it worth for me to keep quiet then?" asked Tumble.

"More than my life's worth!"

"Mmm," mused Tumble as she worked out how much that might be. "Well that would make it about...mmm...let's say, half a pig ear."

"Half a pig ear!" gasped Ruff. "That's far too much! My life is never worth half a pig ear!"

"You said **more** than your life is worth," pointed out Tumble. "Give me half a pig ear or I'll tell the world your secret."

GRRR!

Ruff growled in frustration.

"I'll tell you what, I'll give you half a pig ear providing..."

"Providing what?" asked Tumble, her eyes narrowing in suspicion.

"Providing-that-you-listen-to-my-story," blurted out Ruff in a big rush.

Tumble mumbled and groaned a lot but was secretly quite looking forward to hearing Ruff's story, so she gave in.

"Ok then. Where's my pig ear?"

"Half a pig ear!" protested Ruff.

"Ok! Half a pig ear."

Ruff jumped up and stuck his snout under his fleecy mattress. He rootled around for some time. After a while he popped his head back up.

"Chewy stick? Only slightly chewed and not much fluff."

"No," said Tumble. "We agreed on half a pig ear. You know half a pig ear is worth five chewy sticks of any dog's money. So don't try and trick me."

"Ok!"

Ruff stuck his head back under his mattress. The rootling became more and more frantic, the fleecy mattress

jumping up and down with Ruff's efforts. He stuck his head back up again with a slightly desperate look in his eyes.

"I've got a couple of tripe sticks?" When he saw Tumble's hard stare he added, "And a bowl of Snozzle."

Snozzle was a rather imaginative name that the Pack Leader and Lead Female had given to the dried, husky nuggets of tasteless biscuits that they had to eat at every meal.

Tumble had to admit, at least to herself, that this was quite a good offer.

But watching Ruff squirm is even better. It's worth half a pig ear on its own.

"Look, I'll have to pay you later," said Ruff with a *humph*. "The next time we get pig ears I'll give you half of mine."

"All of it."

"What do you mean 'all of it'? We agreed on half a pig ear!"

"Ah!" said Tumble with a smug grin. "If you don't pay me now then you'll be borrowing it.

And when you borrow you have to pay back more. It's called interest."

"Interest!" gasped Ruff. "If you only had some interest, in my fantastic story, then we wouldn't be having this argument," he mumbled under his breath.

"I heard that!" snapped Tumble.

Ruff scratched behind his ear, trying to remember what they had been talking about before all the looking for half a pig ear began.

A small piece of fir tree dropped into his Night Bed. He stared at it wide-eyed.

"Look, look, look!"

"What?" asked Tumble, bemused.

"It's a piece of fir tree!"

"Ooooo!" exclaimed Tumble in a sarcastic tone.

Ruff gave her a **Look**.

"In my dream I was skiing down a mountain slope and I bashed into some fir trees. I bet this piece of fir tree got stuck in my coat then!"

Tumble rolled her eyes.

This is just the sort of trick that Ruff used to fool me last time.

On their previous 'adventure' Ruff had hidden some of his old toys and produced them one at a time, pretending that they were the Crown Jewels that had gone missing in the ᖴᗩᑎ丂ᗩᔕY ᖇᗴᗩしᗰ.

I don't mind playing along as a game but I don't want to end up actually believing it's real. Not like last time. It was really embarrassing chasing after that goblin and finding out that it was just a tree stump.

"It's just a piece of fir tree," **grumbled** Tumble.

"Yes but I told you there were fir trees in my dream!"

"Ruff, it's just an ordinary piece of fir tree that

you picked up in the **Woods**. One is not going to believe that your dreams are 'real'."

I'm not going to be tricked into believing Ruff's fantasies again. He's always bringing bits of tree back from Walkies in the **Woods**. *His scruffy black coat is like a magnet for twigs and seeds and leaves and stuff. Not like my immaculate, sleek, glossy coat. But then I am a* **Princess**.

"You never believe anything I have to say!" moaned Ruff.

"Yes I do!" protested Tumble. "Last time you had me lured into a whole quest to save the Pack Lands."

"But apparently it was all just my imagination and wasn't real at all. Apparently *I'M* living in a fantasy world. But then I'm just a servant aren't I – **Princess!**"

"What's that supposed to mean?" yapped Tumble.

"What do you want it to mean?" **rumbled** Ruff.

"I DON'T REALLY WANT IT TO MEAN ANYTHING!" snarled Tumble.

"**WELL THAT'S WHAT IT MEANS THEN!**" growled Ruff.

"WELL THAT'S OK THEN!" snapped Tumble.

"**RIGHT!**" barked Ruff.

"RIGHT!" screamed Tumble.

"**Be quiet!**" shouted the Pack Leader from the other side of the Big Bedroom door. This was shortly followed by a thud, a bit like the sound of a slipper bouncing off of a door.

Ruff and Tumble scowled at each other and sunk back into their Night Beds.

Chapter Three

Snow

The next morning Ruff and Tumble **burst** out of the Doggy Doorway into the garden. And skidded to a stop.

Many moons ago, when she was a puppy, Tumble had viciously attacked a can of something called 'shaving foam'.

It wasn't my fault.

She had just suffered her first ever bath and was feeling all frantic and mad. She had been leaping and spinning on the bathroom floor, snarling and tugging at the towel that the Pack Leader was using to ruffling her soaking wet fur dry, when the can of shaving foam had been knocked to the floor.

I snapped it up in my mouth and chomped down really hard. My needle sharp puppy teeth went straight through the can and a load of foul tasting white stuff squirted out. And out and out and out…there was no stopping the stuff. I tried to but the can kept squirming around on the floor, coating everything in a thick layer of white stuff.

The Pack Leader wasn't very pleased.

The garden looks like someone has chomped into the biggest can of shaving foam ever! The ground is all white.

Brrr!

And **COLD**.

"What's all this stuff?" she asked.

"**Snow**," replied Ruff.

"No, neither do I."

Ruff frowned. "What?"

"I don't know what it is either," repeated Tumble.

"No, I said, 𝕤𝕟𝕠𝕨. As in, this stuff is called 𝕤𝕟𝕠𝕨."

This 𝕤𝕟𝕠𝕨 stuff is quite soft, thought Tumble as she stood up to her knees in the ground. She backed up, dragging her legs through the ground, leaving a furrow, like dragging your finger through a pile of spilt flour or sugar.

That's funny! I may be a little…er round... but I don't usually leave a furrow in the ground.

Looking more closely she realised that it wasn't the ground; the ground was underneath the cold, white, soft, 𝕤𝕟𝕠𝕨 stuff.

Mmm, very curious.

She stuck her nose down and sniffed. It didn't smell of anything, except cold, which to a dog's sensitive nose comes in various shades of blue.

Tumble tried to rub some life back into her nose but it didn't really help much because her paws were also numb with cold by now.

She was just thinking about this coldness when something smacked into the back of her head and sprays of the cold, white, soft stuff exploded around her ears. She looked around just in time to catch another ball of cold whiteness right in the face.

Ruff, who had watched the children on the Flickery Light Box With Noises throwing snow at each other the night before, was pelting Tumble with snowballs.

"Hey!" shouted Tumble.

"Hey yourself!" retorted Ruff, hurling a final missile before bounding away.

After running around in the 𝔰𝔫𝔬𝔴 for a while, trying to get some life back into his numb paws, Ruff found that the cold was beginning to chill another part of his body, which was being dragged around underneath him. He cocked his leg and squirted the 𝔰𝔫𝔬𝔴, leaving a Wee Mail about the problem of being a short dog in deep 𝔰𝔫𝔬𝔴 as a warning for other doggies that might come along. Of course, none were likely to come along because they were in the garden but he needed to wee anyway and there was no point wasting it.

Turning to sniff his message, to check the spelling and grammar, he was surprised to see that he had melted a little yellow hole in the 𝕤𝕟𝕠𝕨.

"Hey, Tumble, look at this," he shouted enthusiastically. "If you wee in the 𝕤𝕟𝕠𝕨 it leaves a yellow hole."

"That is gross," said Tumble. "One is not amused by such rudeness, not being a common mutt. One will restrain oneself until this 𝕤𝕟𝕠𝕨 stuff is gone!"

Tumble turned and strutted off, disappearing back into the house through the Doggy Doorway, leaving behind a little brown pile, steaming its way down into the 𝕤𝕟𝕠𝕨.

Ruff watched her go, shrugged and turned his attention back to the yellow hole.

I bet if I was clever I could write my name in the snow.

He sat staring at the small yellow hole thoughtfully, wishing he was clever, until the sound of shouting, squealing children distracted him.

He realised that it had been going on for some time but he hadn't really taken much notice in his excitement at exploring the snow.

It's coming from the neighbouring Pack Lands.

He pushed his way through snowy shrubs, drifts of snow collecting behind his ears, until he got to the slated fence between the Pack Lands.

The two children next door were gleefully hurling snowballs at each other, laughing and howling as they chased each other around their garden. Ruff shouted enthusiastically, asking to join in, but before they had a chance to answer, their Lead Female called them in for lunch.

Lunch, thought Ruff with a sigh. *I wish we had lunch. I could do with a bit of lunch.*

His tummy **rumbled**.

But we have to wait for the Pack Leader to come back from the Daily Hunt before we get anything to eat.

His breakfast bowl of Snozzle and Gravy seemed a long time ago.

He was about to go back indoors, to see if there were any emergency Treats hidden in his

Day Bed, when a flutter of colour caught his eye from the garden beyond the one next door.

What is it?

It was quite a long way away and he couldn't quite make it out.

It would be much easier to see if it was closer. Ah! Closer!

He reached into his Back Pocket and rootled around until he put his paw on a metal tube. He took it out and pulled at one end, stretching the tube longer. The tube had a glass lens at each end, one end narrower than the other. Ruff put the smaller of the two ends to his eye and peered through it.

My Secret Agent Bring Things Closer So You Can See Them Better Device will do the trick.

The telescope didn't actually bring anything closer, it just seemed that way, but Ruff could now see that the fluttering colourful thing was a scarf, blowing in the breeze. The scarf was wrapped around the neck of a...

ARGGGHHHH!!
Yeti! It's a Dog Eating Yeti!!

The **Dog Eating Yeti** was also wearing a woolly hat. Its arms looked like sticks and it had a curious, pointy, orange nose.

And it's eyes are as black as a black cat's **EVIL** *black heart!*

"**BEGONE, BEGONE, BEGONE!!**" shouted Ruff.

But the **Dog Eating Yeti** took no notice. In fact it didn't even move.

It's like it's frozen in place, just staring through the fence, straight at the Pack Lands! It's spying on us!

Ruff turned and hurtled towards the house. He clattered through the Doggy Doorway into the kitchen, dragging **SNOW** and cold air in with him.

Tumble was sat in her Day Bed. Her head darted around at the sound of the Doggy Doorway, her eyes big and round, ears flat to her head. Hanging from her jaw was a bag of crisps.

"**THE Yetis ARE HERE!   THE Yetis ARE HERE!**" shouted Ruff.

Tumble dropped the bag of crisps into her bed and pushed it under her fleecy mattress as quietly as possible. Being a **crunchy** bag of crisps, this wasn't very quietly.

Ruff didn't seem to notice. He was skipping around on the floor, still barking, "**THE Yetis ARE HERE!   THE Yetis ARE HERE!**"

"What are you yelling about!" snapped Tumble.

"**THE Yetis ARE HERE!**" shouted Ruff, right in Tumble's ear. He was amazed that she hadn't heard him.

I can't shout it any louder!

"The **Dog Eating Yetis** I was telling you about! They've come to invade the Pack Lands!"

53

Tumble bashed a paw against her ear and shook her head, trying to clear the ringing noise from it.

"I thought you said the Dog Eating Yetis were trying to take over the FANTASY REALM. You didn't say anything about the Pack Lands!"

"Tumble! That was in my book. It was just a story. This is real life! They're here, they're here!"

"Ruff, just be quiet for a minute and tell me about it!"

Ruff jumped into his bed and stared up at the kitchen clock. He fidgeted about, stared at Tumble and then back at the clock. He hopped up and down, scuffed up his fleecy mattress a bit, circled round and round, plonked himself down, glanced up at the clock again, then stared wide eyed at the

Doggy Doorway, whimpering slightly.

From beyond the Doggy Doorway came the sound of the children next door charging back out into their garden to play. It should have been a reassuring sound but Ruff continued to whimper.

Tumble waited patiently whilst all this was going on, then said, "What are you doing? I thought you were going to tell me about it!"

Ruff frowned and looked pointedly at the clock and back at Tumble.

Tumble raised her eyebrows and rolled her eyes skyward, or at least ceilingward. "It's just a phrase Ruff; something people say without meaning it. You don't  actually have to be quiet for a minute!"

"Oh right!" said Ruff sitting up in his bed, his tail wagging. "The Yetis are here! Or did I say that already? I did, didn't I. Well, they are here and they're going to suck the life out of everyone."

"Ruff, that is just your book again!"

"No it's not! You didn't let me tell you about my dream last night. You distracted me by tricking me out of half a pig ear. I was *Righteous Rufus*, a.k.a. James Bone, **OO-LOTS**, licensed to kill and..."

"What does a.k.a. mean?" interrupted Tumble.

"It's **SECRET AGENT** code, it stands for 'also known as'. Anyway, I was on a secret mission. I had broken into the Yetis secret base and stolen..."

"How did you know where it was, if it was secret?" interrupted Tumble, again.

"Because, I'm a **SECRET AGENT**, that knows secret stuff and does secret things," whispered Ruff, his eyes darting left and right.

Tumble leant forward, a slight frown on her brow, eyes also searching the shadows. "So what had you stolen?"

"The Yetis secret plan!"

Tumble's eyes widened, intrigued. "What did it say?"

"Their plan was to send snow and ICE to freeze the FANTASY REALM and then, when everyone was frozen they'd attack and suck their life out!"

Tumble SNORTED. "That's a very simple plan, doesn't sound like much of a cunning EVIL plot to me."

"Simple but deadly," said Ruff. "Because once everyone has had their life sucked out they won't be able to fight back will they."

"Mmm," mumbled Tumble through pursed lips. "It's a good point. Maybe it's a more cunning EVIL plan that I thought. But that's got nothing to do with us, has it. That's in the FANTASY REALM."

"I think it might be real!" Ruff gave a little

grelp and glanced at the Doggy Doorway.

Tumble found her own eyes drawn to the Doggy Doorway. It swung inwards and a few flakes of snow billowed in with the wind.

Tumble backed a little deeper into her Day Bed, keeping an eye on the Doggy Doorway. "Why do you think it might be real?"

"Because the Pack Lands have been filled with snow and ICE!"

Tumble found she had no answer for that.

It's true!

"And I found that bit of fir tree in my fur last night after my dream. That proves it's real!"

Alarm bells began to ring in Tumble's head now. She clearly remembered thinking that Ruff had put that bit of fir tree in his bed to trick her.

And he nearly did!

"Rubbish! You're just trying to trick me!"

Ruff frowned. "Then how do you explain the Yeti in the garden two Pack Lands away that is secretly watching us?"

"There isn't one," said Tumble settling in a more relaxed position in her Day Bed. "And if there was how would *you* know, if he was doing it secretly!"

"Hah! That just proves my point!" snapped Ruff jumping to his paws.

"Does it?"

"Yes, because I must be a **real SECRET AGENT** if I know secret stuff and if I'm a **real SECRET AGENT** then it follows that everything else is **real**!"

Ruff was very pleased with that argument. Until he realised that it meant there was a **real** Dog Eating Yeti watching the Pack Lands.

Chapter Four

Lunch

Ruff sat in his Day Bed, staring at the Doggy Doorway, worrying.

*What am I going to do if there **iʃ** an invasion of **Dog Eating Yetis?** I can't tackle them all on my own. I don't even know how to fight a Yeti. They look awfully big and I'm only small.*

Perhaps Tumble will help if things get too desperate.

He glanced over at Tumble, who was lying on her back in her Day Bed with all four paws pointing in the air.

*I wish I could relax like that! But how can I with an army of **Dog Eating Yetis** about to smash down the Garden Gate?*

A loud **rumbling** from his

tummy reminded him how **HUNGRY** he was and how much his life lacked lunch. He stood up and started rucking his fleecy cushion up, hunting for anything he could eat amongst the fluff. He huffed and puffed and grelped and yowled, getting more and more desperate. In the end, he stuck his nose under the cushion and flipped the whole thing out onto the floor.

"Will you be quiet for a minute? I'm trying to sleep here!"

Ruff frowned and then decided that this was just one of those phrases that people say but don't really mean. "I'm **HUNGRY!**" he complained.

"And leaping up and down, spinning around in your bed and tossing your cushion onto the floor helps does it?"

"I'm looking for something to eat!"

"What, in your bed? How disgusting," growled Tumble. She rolled over to give Ruff a **Look** and loudly **crunched** the bag of crisps, still hidden under her cushion.

Ruff's ears pricked up at the sound. "What have you got there, Tumble?"

"Nothing!" lied Tumble.

"Sounds like crisps," suggested Ruff.

"What sounds like crisps?" hedged Tumble.

"That appetising **crunching** noise," said Ruff.

"What appetising **crunching** noise?" asked Tumble, sweating a little.

"The one coming from your bed," said Ruff.

"I don't know what you are talking about, Ruff. It's not like the Pack Leader dropped a bag of crisps on the kitchen floor this morning, which I was quick to rescue and hide in my bed so I could eat them later when you weren't looking. I mean, what are the chances of that happening?" babbled tumble, finishing with a fixed grin.

"Can I have half?"

"Oh! Ok then!" agreed Tumble, giving up under Ruff's tough questioning. "But you'll owe me half a bag of crisps, Ok?"

"Fine," agreed Ruff.

"I mean you'll owe me half a bag of crisps and the half a pig ear that you already owe me," Tumble added.

"Ok," said Ruff, "I'll tell you what. To make things simple, if you give me half of the crisps that you have now then I'll owe you half of my crisps when I've got some."

Tumble furrowed her brow but couldn't see anything wrong with this. "*And* the half a pig ear?"

"Of course," agreed Ruff, happy that Tumble seem to have forgotten the half a pig ear interest.

"Ok." Tumble stood on the crisp packet causing it to **burst** open, spraying crisps across the floor. There was a scurry of paws and claws as the dogs gathered half each.

Tumble munched away happily on her pile and had soon **DEMOLISHED** them. Ruff however, despite his tummy **rumbling** in protest, sat with his pile untouched before him.

It wasn't long before Tumble began eyeing out Ruff's pile with desperate longing. Ruff waited until Tumble began to **DRIBBLE** slightly before making an offer.

"Would you like some of my crisps, Tumble?"

"Oh, yes please!" said Tumble.

"Well, if I give you half of my crisps that will pay you back for the crisps I borrowed from you."

Tumble tried to think about this.

She had a feeling that something was wrong with the deal but she couldn't put her claw on it.

It sounds right. And I am really **HUNGRY**.

"Ok."

Ruff divided his pile of crisps in two and nudged one half over to Tumble. Once again Tumble devoured them in an instant. It wasn't long before she was staring at Ruff's pile and **DRIBBLING** again.

"Would you like some of my crisps, Tumble?"

"Oh, yes please!" said Tumble.

"Well, seeing as I owe you **half** a pig ear how about if I paid you back with **half** of my crisps."

Tumble was beyond thinking hard now.

*Sooo **HUNGRY!** Ruff is offering me half of something for half of something else. That must be a fair deal...*

I've got to have those crisps!

"Ok, I agree. Now give me the crisps!"

Ruff divided his crisps once more and nosed half over to Tumble. This time Ruff quickly munched through his pile as quickly as Tumble. He didn't want Tumble finishing and getting any more.

As he dozed off to sleep he felt very pleased with himself. *I didn't get to eat many crisps but they were free, because I paid Tumble back for them. And I managed to pay off my debt of half a pig ear!*

So, whilst there weren't many crisps, they had tasted particularly fine.

He had also completely forgotten about the **Dog Eating Yeti** watching the Pack Lands.

Chapter Five

Lots of Questions

The Pack Leader and the Lead Female had come back from the Daily Hunt early. They had whisked Ruff and Tumble up and bundled them onto the back seat of the **NOISY METAL BOX THAT TRANSPORTS**. They were now jabbering excitedly away to each other as the car slowly ploughed its way along the snow buried roads.

Ruff was also jabbering excitedly; at Tumble. He was telling her about the dream he had just had. *Righteous Rufus*, a.k.a. James Bone, had set off on a dangerous mission to stop the advance of the Dog Eating Yetis.

But Tumble refused to jabber excitedly back. In fact, Ruff wasn't even sure she was listening.

"Look! This is important! If *Righteous Rufus* can find a way to defeat the **Dog Eating Yetis** then we'll be safe!"

"I think we are fairly safe anyway," replied Tumble. "Your 'dream' is taking place in the **ᖴᗩᑎᗷᗩᔕY ᖇEᗩᒪᗰ**, not the real world. There aren't any **Dog Eating Yetis** here."

"Yes there are! What about the one I saw two Pack Lands away?"

"I don't think it's real," said Tumble.

"Of course it's real! It was stood there secretly watching our Pack Lands."

"*I* didn't see it."

"*You* didn't look!" growled Ruff. "Anyway, that piece of fir tree we found in my Night Bed proves it's real. I dreamt about Whizzy Snow Gliding down a mountain and bashing through some fir trees and then a piece of fir tree ends up in my bed. It must be real.

How else could it have got there?"

"Perhaps some sneaky Scottie hid it there to try and fool me into another daft dream adventure," suggested Tumble.

"I didn't hide it! It's real!"

"It is not real, it is just a dream and you'll not talk me into believing otherwise."

"But it's real!"

And that was the secret of how Ruff won arguments. There was nothing overly clever about it, in fact every toddling human child is an expert. You just keep repeating what you think, or want, over and over again until the other person cracks.

But Tumble knew how to deal with it. She stuck her paws in her ears and chanted, "Nanana-Ican'thearyou-nananana…"

After a while she stopped chanting and extracted a paw.

"IT'S REAL!" snapped Ruff.

71

"NA NA NA NA NA NA NA NA NA..."

Ruff *humphed*.

There's no point trying to have a sensible talk with Tumble when she's in this kind of mood.

"NA NA NA NA NA NA NA NA NA NA..."

"Be quiet in the back will you!" shouted the Pack Leader over the loud growling coming from the back seat of the car.

Tumble was quiet but gave Ruff a stern **Look** for getting her into trouble with the Pack Leader. Ruff scowled back and whispered, just loud enough for Tumble to hear, "It's real!"

Tumble glared at him. Ruff glared back.

"...extremely frosty atmosphere in this unusual cold snap."

Ruff gave a little **parp** of surprise before realising that it was just the strange Voice that sometimes appeared in the **NOISY METAL**

72

BOX THAT TRANSPORTS. He had tried to hunt it down once but all he had found out was that it hid somewhere behind the back seat. With Tumble's help he had managed to sneak a look in the boot but there hadn't been anybody there. Since then he had given up on finding it. He wouldn't have understood what a radio was anyway.

"Well if you're not going to talk about my dream, what are we going to do?" huffed Ruff, trying to shut the Voice out.

"We don't have to *do* anything. Why can't you just be patient? Sit back and enjoy the drive."

Ruff sighed and sat back. But he couldn't be patient; he didn't have the patience for it. And he didn't enjoy the ride.

It wouldn't be so bad if I could see where I was going.

He stood on his tip-claws, trying to look out of the window. He sat back down with a *humph*.

The Voice was still droning on about how cold it was for early autumn, blaming something called **GLOBAL WARMING**.

That's just stupid. How can something warm make it cold. They didn't think that idea through very well. Anyway, it's the Dog Eating Yetis and their secret plan that are to blame.

He heaved himself to his paws and, after turning around and around trying to flatten the long grass on the back seat, plomped back down again. Of course there wasn't really any long grass on the back seat. It was a habit passed down from his ancestors who used to live in the **wilds**, in the days before they tamed humans.

It wasn't long before he gave a **parp** of boredom.

"Do you have to be so common and vulgar?"

"No, but I'm bored," said Ruff and then made a point of **parping** even more loudly.

"You are a rude mongrel who smells like a pig – which is the only good thing about you."

"No. I'm a rude mongrel *who is bored* and smells like a pig. And you're a stuck up snob."

"One is not a stuck up snob," said Tumble, sniffing her dislike for all things common and muttish. "But clearly there will be no peace until you're tiny mind is doing something. So what do you what to do?"

Ruff was a bit insulted by that.

The only reason Tumble can sit around doing nothing is because she's the one with a tiny mind. I, being far more intelligent, need lots of things to keep my much larger brain busy. Which was quite a complex thought for a dog with only three Brain Cells.

"Oh, I know! Why don't we talk about those dreams that aren't really dreams?" asked Ruff in a hopeful tone.

"No!"

"Oh, all right then!" huffed Ruff with a dramatic sigh. "What about a game of something?"

"Ooo, yes!" said Tumble, showing some interest for the first time. *I'm good at games.*

"What shall we play?"

"I don't know," said Ruff.

Scratch scratch.

"How about...Lots of Questions?"

The human version of this game is called Twenty Questions but dogs aren't very good with numbers above three.

"Ok," agreed Tumble. "Bagsie go first!" she added hurriedly, before Ruff had the chance.

Ruff SNORTED in protest but really he was happy to be doing something other than just sitting around.

"Animal, vegetable or mineral?" asked Ruff, starting with the normal first question.

"I don't know but at a guess I'd say that you were a vegetable. Probably a turnip."

Ruff gave Tumble a sneer to show her that she wasn't funny. "Is the thing that you're thinking about an animal, a vegetable or a mineral?"

"Yes!" said Tumble triumphantly.

"What do you mean 'yes'?"

"I only have to answer yes or no," answered Tumble primly.

"Not on the first question you don't, do you?"

"Yes! And that's two questions."

"Come on! That's not fair. Surely you're

cheating now?"

"No! Hah! And that's lots – I win!"

"Hang on! I get a few more goes than that don't I?"

"No! Hah! You're useless at this!"

"**OK!**" snapped Ruff, exasperated at Tumble's behaviour. "Let's play again."

"I go again though, because I won."

"**OK, OK!**" growled Ruff.

"**RIGHT!**"

"**RIGHT!**"

"**WELL GO ON THEN.**"

"**WELL GO ON THEN, WHAT?**" snapped Ruff.

"**ASK A QUESTION!**"

"Oh yes. Animal, vegetable or... Is it a mineral?"

"Yes," growled Tumble, annoyed that Ruff had guessed correctly.

"What colour is it?" asked Ruff.

"Yes! Hahaha!"

"Oh."

This is going to be more difficult than I thought.

Ruff looked about for inspiration and his eyes settled on Tumble's fur. "Is it brown?" he asked.

"Yes," answered Tumble, her brow furrowed in frustration.

That was a good guess. What other questions can I ask?

Ruff **scratched** behind his ear to try and kick start his Brain Cells.

"Hurry up!" interrupted Tumble.

"Ok, Ok! Keep your fur on. It's hard."

"No."

"Yes it is. It's really hard."

"No it isn't! In fact it's quite soft," snapped Tumble.

"Soft?" queried Ruff. "Don't you mean easy?"

Tumble frowned and gave Ruff a dark **Look**. "What are you talking about?"

"Yes!" said Ruff, very confused by now. "Hah!"

Tumble's frown deepened into a scowl. "Look! It's a soft, brown mineral ok?"

"Ah! Right," said Ruff. "Soft and brown…soft and brown…"

Well I can think of **something** *that's soft and brown. But I should ask a couple more questions to make sure before guessing.*

"Does it smell nice?"

"Gorgeous!" said Tumble breaking away from her strict rule of yes/no answers. She had a dreamy look in her eyes. "All rich and dark, especially when it's freshly made."

Ha! thought Ruff. *Tumble gave me more information than she was meant to there. Let's see; something that smells nice, is rich and dark and is something that is made? Well, seeing as it is Tumble thinking about it it's most likely something you can eat.*

"Is it tasty?" he asked.

"Delicious!" said Tumble, her eyes starting to glaze.

Then the glaze hardened and she snapped, "Come on you've had lots of questions already. You have to guess now. And if you're wrong it will be my go again."

"Ok, Ok! Just one more question."

I think I know what it is. I just need to check one more thing.

"Is it light and fluffy?"

"Yes it is, if it's made just right," answered Tumble. "But it's delicious even if it isn't," she added wistfully.

Whilst Tumble was in this dreamy state Ruff sneaked in one more question, "Does it begin with 'C'?"

"What? Oh, no. It begins with K."

Ruff shoulders slumped.

Oh! I thought it was chocolate mousse. But that begins with C. Blast!

Then she remembered playing 'I Spy' with Tumble during their last adventure. They had been in the *NOISY METAL BOX THAT TRANSPORTS* on the way to the

Woods to find **Goblins**.

Ha! Tumble thinks lots of words begin with K when they actually begin with C. Like cat and cow and castle. So she's probably got it wrong this time too!

Ruff grinned the grin of the victorious and made his guess. "Is it a chocolate mousse?" He stretched back on the seat waiting to see Tumble's face drop in disappointment at losing.

"No! I win! My go again. Ha ha!!"

Ruff's face dropped in disappointment at losing. He couldn't believe he was wrong. "Hang on!" he said. "You've got to tell me what the answer is."

"Cowpat," said Tumble.

"COWPAT? COWPAT? WHAT DO YOU...," began Ruff. But he was cut short because the **NOISY METAL BOX THAT TRANSPORTS** had come to a stop. They had arrived.

Chapter Six

Invasion of the Dog Eating Yetis

Both dogs leapt out of the **NOISY METAL BOX THAT TRANSPORTS**, eager to use up some of their Beans. They were so Full of Beans that they were fit to explode. They had to get rid of some of them quickly.

But they didn't race around in a **burst** of Beans as they had planned. They stood chest deep in snow.

Ruff's eyes widened in **HORROR**. They were high up on Dartmoor and as far as he could see, in every direction, the land was covered in snow. It was so white it made his eyes hurt.

Poopscoops! The dog eating Yetis' secret plan is working! It's not just the Pack Lands; they've covered the whole world in snow! Next they'll swarm across the land and kill everyone! We're doomed!

Whomp!

Snow **burst** across his nose and into his eyes.

"ARRGGH!"

"Yeti ATTACK, Yeti ATTACK!!" cried Ruff.

But it was only a snowball hurled by Tumble.

As another one flew his way, Ruff forgot his worries about the Dog Eating Yetis, dodged the missile and chased after Tumble.

They raced around, dodging between other Packs that were out on the Moors enjoying the snow. They barked and growled and snapped and hurled snowballs at each other, quickly using up their Beans.

After a few minutes they stopped for a rest, their breath puffing out in clouds to hang before them in the windless air. They sat side by side next to a large, snow draped stone cross, one of the few things in the landscape that wasn't entirely white.

It started to snow again. Ruff watched, cross-eyed, as the snow began to pile up on his nose. It tickled. He sneezed, scattering the pile but it soon began to heap up again.

Ignoring it he looked up at the sky. It was now as white as the ground. It was confusing having everything white. It was hard to work out where everything was and how far away it was.

Like burrowing under the white duvet cover on the Big Bed. It would be nice to have some colour.

"Do you think, it if was sunny, that there would be a snowbow?" he asked.

Tumble turned her head to frown at Ruff. "What's a snowbow?"

"Well," began Ruff, "when there's **rain** and sun at the same time you get a **rain**bow, so maybe if there's **snow** and sun together you'd get a **snow**bow."

"Pah!" SNORTED Tumble. "That's nonsense! If the sun came out and shone on this cross here," said Tumble, indicating the

large stone cross sticking out of the 𝕊𝕟𝕠𝕨 next to them, "you wouldn't get a *cross*bow would you."

Ruff frowned. "That's not the same at all. If..."

Seeing that Ruff was going to start some long winded explanation about his ideas on snowbows, Tumble quickly interrupted, "Hey look, what are the Pack Leader and Lead Female up to?"

Still frowning, Ruff turned his head to look in the Pack Leader and Lead Females' direction. His frown deepened. *Mmmm? What are they up to?*

They were pushing a massive ball of 𝕊𝕟𝕠𝕨 across the ground.

Are they trying to make the biggest snowball ever? That's stupid: they'll never be able to throw it. Even a __troll__ wouldn't be able to throw it. Not even a whole __trolley of trolls__.

There, I was right. They've made it so big they've just had to leave it lying there. The Pack Lead and Lead Female had left the huge ball of snow and wandered over to a fresh patch of snow.

Ruff smiled to himself: *I'm so clever.*

Oh no! They're making another one now.

Ruff watched the Lead Female pushing a ball of __snow__ across the ground, leaving a green strip of freshly uncovered grass behind it. Once it reached about a quarter of the size of the first ball she stopped.

Ah! They're learning.

But it's still too big to throw.

"See! I was right," said Ruff, nudging Tumble in the ribs with his elbow. "They can barely lift it, let alone throw it!"

Tumble gave him a funny look. She wasn't sure what Ruff was supposed to be right about. She hadn't been part of the sad little conversation in his head.

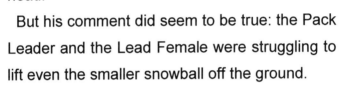

But his comment did seem to be true: the Pack Leader and the Lead Female were struggling to lift even the smaller snowball off the ground.

Finally, with a grunt of effort, they managed to haul it off the ground. Staggering a few feet under its weight, they plonked it on top of the first, larger snowball.

Ruff got up and sauntered over to the double snowball thing. Or, rather, he ploughed through the snow in a saunter-like way. He sniffed it. It smelt blue.

What is it supposed to be?

Meanwhile, the Pack Leader had found a couple of sticks and he thrust one of these in each side of the larger, bottom snowball.

Ruff still wasn't impressed but sat down to see what else might happen.

Tumble wandered over and sat down beside him, also wondering what was going on.

The Lead Female had taken off her hat and scarf. She wound the scarf around the join between the two snowballs and plonked the hat on top of the smaller one.

Ruff frowned.

Surely this thing isn't meant to be some kind of hat stand is it? What a waste of time. Why doesn't the Lead Female just fold up her hat and scarf and put them in her Back Pocket, like any sensible dog would?

Ruff was about to wander off and find some proper entertainment when the Pack Leader produced a carrot from his pocket. Ruff decided to stick around to see what he was going to do with it.

The Pack Leader poked two holes in the smaller snowball with the carrot and then stuck it into the snowball just below the midpoint between the two holes.

Ruff and Tumble leapt to their paws, hackles raised and growling deep in their chests. They backed away cautiously, until they were at a safe distance, and then began to raise the alarm.

"**ALARM ALARM ALARM!!!**" shouted Ruff.

"**ABOMINABLE SNOWMAN, ABOMINABLE SNOWMAN, ABOMINABLE SNOWMAN!!!**" barked Tumble.

"Yeti, Yeti, Yeti!!" shouted Ruff, which was a lot easier to bark.

Unfortunately none of this seemed to do much good.

Firstly, the Yeti didn't run away with its tail between its legs. Of course it didn't actually have a tail – or any legs – but the important thing is that it didn't run away.

Secondly, the Pack Leader and Lead Female had totally ignored their warning. In fact, they were stood right next to the Dog Eating Yeti, laughing at them!

And thirdly, the other Packs who were out and about enjoying the snow weren't rushing to help.

Tumble, who couldn't believe that a real Dog Eating Yeti had actually turned up, glanced around to see why no one was coming to help them.

"ARRGH! THE Yetis ARE EVERYWHERE!"

She was right. The Packs all about them seemed to have their own Yetis to deal with.

We're going to have to defeat this one on our own.

They watched the Yeti warily. It hadn't attacked yet. It was playing things cool. Well it would, wouldn't it?

It's probably waiting to see what they we're going to do, thought Ruff. *Great! That gives us time to plan.*

"Right!" growled Ruff, still watching the Yeti cautiously. "What shall we do?"

"I don't know," said Tumble. "What do you

think we should do?"

"Well, I'll go in from the front and you circle around and approach it from the rear. Then, once we have it surrounded, we'll...we'll fall upon it! And once we've got it pinned down we'll...we'll..."

"We'll what?" asked Tumble, a slight frown creasing her brow. She was remembering a plan that had started just like this one, when they had been trying to stop the **Invasion of the Goblin Horde** a little while ago.

Ruff convinced me that there were goblins in the Woods. Being very brave I volunteered to herd them up. And ended up being laughed at for herding a tree stump!

"Well, we'll...er...we'll...I'm sure we'll know what to do once we've pinned it down," mumbled Ruff, a bit annoyed that he was having to do all the thinking. "Do you have a better plan?" he added, a little snappily.

Tumble didn't like Ruff's tone but didn't want to admit that she didn't have **any** plan, let alone a better plan.

"I suppose we could attack all of them," said Ruff, sweeping his paw out to point at all the Yetis around them. "Then you could herd them up - like tree stumps. You're good at that."

"THAT WASN'T MY FAULT! YOU TOLD ME THE TREE STUMP WAS A GOBLIN!" shouted Tumble.

"**OK!**" growled Ruff, stepping around in front of Tumble to stand nose to nose with her. "**IT WAS AN EASY MISTAKE TO MAKE. DON'T GET YOUR TAIL IN A TANGLE.**"

That was just too much for Tumble, whose tail was *never* in a tangle. She snapped and flew at Ruff in a snarling flurry of teeth and claws.

But Ruff was expecting the attack and quickly stepped aside, leaving Tumble charging at the Yeti. In her blind fury Tumble didn't care; she was going to take it out on someone and the Yeti, though second choice to Ruff right now, would have to do.

Tumble fell upon her foe with fang and fury. She leapt up as high as she could and sunk her sharp teeth into the warm flesh of its neck. Ripping its jugular vein she felt its rich life blood spurt from the terrible wound.

Well, that was the plan anyway. What really happened was that its head fell off, spilling the scarf, hat and carrot to the ground.

Tumble skipped about in the ꙅꞑꞻ, very confused.

Where has the Dog Eating Yeti gone! It was here. I killed it! But now there are just these great big snowballs that the Pack Leader and Lead Female made.

Ruff sauntered over. "Snowballs eh!"

Tumble **Looked** at her.

"Quite vicious I understand."

Tumble started a low growl deep down in her chest.

"They can give you a nasty bite – frostbite! Hahaha!"

"The growl began to climb out of Tumble's chest, getting louder with each passing moment.

"Herded them, did you?"

Tumble fell upon her foe with fang and fury.

But her foe was already skipping through the snow **parping** in delight.

Chapter Seven

Screelers, Incas and Fat Bellied Pigs

Ruff and Rainbow Lion were perched on top of the big soft comfy thing looking out of the window, being Vitally Vigilant. It was snowing heavily; a never ending cascade of big, fluffy flakes drifting down to cover the ground in an ever thickening blanket of white.

Ruff stared out into the whiteness trying to spot any Dog Eating Yetis that might be sneaking up on the Pack Lands.

How am I supposed to spot a beast that is white sneaking up in all this whiteness? Oh! What about my Secret Agent Bring Things Closer So You Can See Them Better Device?

Ruff checked over his shoulder to make sure no one was watching. The Pack Leader and the Lead Female were busy watching the Flickery Light Box With Noises and Tumble was curled up next to them, asleep. He carefully eased the telescope from his Back Pocket and peered through it.

Blast! Everything is closer but it's still all white! I can't see a thing. It might as well be dark!

Oh! Dark! I could use my new See Clearly When Its Dark (Even If It's All A Bit Green) Devices.

Now that he was a **SECRET AGENT** Ruff had decided that he needed a few gadgets and had ordered some night vision binoculars from

the Internet.

Shoving the telescope into his Back Pocket he rootled around a bit and then pulled out the binoculars. When he looked through them everything became eerily green, like those television programmes where they watch badgers or hedgehogs at night.

This is useless. Now it's just all green instead of white. I still can't see anything!

Ruff humphed. Giving up on being Vitally Vigilant, he shuffled around to watch the Flickery Light Box With Noises.

The Pack Leader and Lead Female were watching some boring programme about an ancient tribe known as Incas. They came from

a far away land and built triangular houses called pyramids. They also had massive stone temples where they worshiped their Sun God: Inti. But apparently, whilst they had a vast empire and were very civilised and intelligent, they had been defeated by a small pack of Spaniels.

Ruff got bored and turned back to check on the progress of the Invasion of the Dog Eating Yetis.

The snow had stopped falling, so at least he could now see beyond the low fence separating the Pack Lands from the pavement and road beyond. He peered up and down the road. There were no Dog Eating Yetis to be seen.

But they are masters of camouflage! They'll blend in with the background and I won't see them even if they are there.

Ruff stared dutifully up and down the road. But there wasn't much going on. A couple of humans were scrunching slowly through the deep snow and a flurry of children went past throwing

snowballs at each other. But that was all.

Ruff's head was just sagging to the soft, fluffiness of the top of the 𝔹𝕚𝕘 𝕊𝕠𝕗𝕥 𝕔𝕠𝕞𝕗𝕪 𝕥𝕙𝕚𝕟𝕘, his heavy eyelids dragging closed, when there was a terrific explosion of noise and light!

Ruff leapt to his paws and barked a warning to the Pack.

WE ARE UNDER ATTACK!

WE ARE UNDER ATTACK!!

GUARD THE DOORS!

BARRICADE THE GATES!!

The Pack Leader joined in with a growly warning to the invading Dog Eating Yetis: **BE QUIET!**

But all Tumble did was raise one eyelid and mutter, "It's just a snowball Ruff."

Ruff stopped mid bark, frowning. He looked at the window. There was a large, circular patch of snow squashed against it that was slowly sliding down the glass. Beyond were the children from the Pack Lands next to them, pointing and laughing.

Humph!

Ruff turned his back on them.

There was a different programme on the Flickery Light Box With Noises now. It was about pigs.

Little pigs with big fat tummies.

"Hey, Ruff," said Tumble from the cushions below, "if we shaved your shaggy black coat off you'd look just like one of those."

Ruff SNORTED in disgust and Beamed at the Pack Leader, *Change the programme, change the programme...*

The Pack leader absentmindedly picked up the remote control and stabbed at a button. The programme changed.

Ruff stood up in amazement at the sight in front of him on the Flickery Light Box with Noises.

Magnificent!

A young boy was whizzing up and down ramps, somersaulting and twisting over jumps and sliding down rails on a...on a...something.

What is it? It got two bits; a flat bit, a little like a...a flat thing, and a bit underneath with wheels, like a...a wheelie thing.

Ruff scratched behind his ear to get his third Brain Cell working.

Ok, Ok. A flat thing. The only flat thing I can think of is a scrubbing board. But what about the wheelie thing? Ohhh, ohhh, a roller skate. Yes, that's good. So, it's a Scrubbing Board Roller Skate. Mmm, bit of a mouthful perhaps? What about a boardskate? No, that sounds stupid, like an uninterested fish. A scrubbing roller? A scruboller? Ah, a scroller! No. It sounds a bit slow, like a stroller, and that thing is zipping about the place really fast.

Ruff sat down again. This was going to take a lot of thought, not usual for a Scottie.

Maybe it's not a roller skate for the wheelie thing. Maybe just wheelie thing? Or wheeler! That would make a scrub wheeler. A scrubeeler. Ohhh, ohhh! A Screeler! Yes! It's a Screeler! Look at the way it's screeling down those rails!

Ruff sneaked his pad and pencil from his Back Pocket and flicked through the pages until he found his Wish List. Licking the pencil end he added, '1 x Screeler'.

Ruff watched the skateboarders on the TV as they performed all sorts or crazy flips and jumps, twisting and spinning in the air until the Pack Leader switched it off. Ruff was twitching with excitement.

Screeler riders are awesome!

Then he frowned.

But they do crash quite a lot.

He opened his notepad again and added '4 x kneepads' and '1 x helmet' to his wish list. Then he crossed out '1 x helmet' and put an arrow pointing to his earlier scribble about the Whizzy Snow Glider. He wrote, 'just need 1 helmet'.   Then, as an afterthought, he added, '1 x cool T-shirt with a skull and stuff on it to match helmet'.

He was about to write, 'Again, not a <u>real</u> skull!' when he realised the Pack Leader had switched off the Flickery Light Box With Noises. He quickly stuffed his notepad back in his pocket before the Pack Leader could turn

around and spot him.

Just in time!

"Ok doggies. Time for Final Wee Wees in the garden."

Ruff scrambled from the 𝐛𝐢𝐠 𝐬𝐨𝐟𝐭 𝐜𝐨𝐦𝐟𝐲 𝐭𝐡𝐢𝐧𝐠 and out through the Doggy Doorway into the garden with Tumble. Final Wee Wees performed they rushed up the stairs and settled into their Night Beds.

As Ruff drifted off to sleep his mind whirred away, flashing images of Screelers, fat bellied pigs, the Incas and their Sun God.

Chapter Eight

Squealer Games

When the Pack Leader opened the Big Bedroom Door the next morning, Ruff woke instantly; bright, alert and excited. He raced to the top of the stairs and hopped from  paw to paw, waiting for the Pack Leader to open the gate that stopped them roaming around the Pack Lands at night.

The moment the gate was opened the merest crack, Ruff shoved his nose, head and then shoulders through. Barging the gate wide open he nearly tumbled the Pack Leader down the stairs in his rush.

Ruff raced down the stairs, paws barely touching them in his flight. Before the Pack Leader had taken three steps, Ruff was already through the lounge and kitchen and had clunked through the Doggy Doorway into the garden.

And there he stood, chest deep in snow looking completely deflated, all his bright puffiness gone.

Why is all the snow still here? And where is the sun? It's still all cloudy. I thought Righteous Rufus, had saved the Fantasy Realm. I thought that meant the Pack Lands would be saved too.

Ruff had dreamt that Righteous Rufus had completed his secret mission. He had brought the sun back to melt all the ICE and snow in the Fantasy Realm, stopping the Invasion of the Dog Eating Yetis.

But all the snow is still here!

Ruff humphed

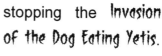

loudly.

I wonder if the Dog Eating Yeti two Pack Lands down is still watching us?

Ruff ploughed his way through the 🅢🅝🅞🅦 towards the slated fence between the Pack Lands. He pushed through the shrubs, 🅢🅝🅞🅦 dropping onto his shaggy coat, and peered through a gap.

ARRRGGHHH!

The Yeti two gardens away **was** still there, he could see its scarf flapping in the breeze. But what had really alarmed him was the Dog Eating Yeti stood just the other side of the fence!

Luckily it wasn't looking in his direction. With a nervous growlp he crouched down low, lying flat in the snow to keep out of sight but still ready to run if necessary. He studied his foe through the fence.

The Yeti was a bit misshapen, with a very small head for the size of its body. It had a plastic bucket upturned on its head as a hat and its nose looked like a clothes peg. One arm was gnarly and stick-like whilst the other was incredibly straight and thin with a very colourful hand.

It looks like one of those brightly coloured plastic windmill things that spin in the wind. Freaky!

A gust of icy air skipped over the Pack Lands next door, flicking twirling spirals of snow into the air. It squeezed through the gaps in the fence and rippled through Ruff's fur, sending a shiver down his back.

ARRGH! ITS HAND IS SPINNING!

Maybe it isn't its hand? Maybe it's holding a

deadly ninja throwing star!

Ruff cringed back into the shrubs out of sight. Peering through the leaves he was relieved to see that the throwing star had stopped spinning. He studied the Yeti's face and decided that it still wasn't looking at him.

Its eyes are a bit wonky though. One eye seems to be looking at the Back Portal of the house next door but the other is staring at our Back Portal! And the Doggy Doorway! It wants to suck the life out of us!

There was another gust of icy air and the Yeti's throwing star started to spin again.

Poopscoops!

Ruff slowly backed out through the shrubs, gathering more snow in his fur, behind his ears and down his snout. When he was sure he was out of sight he made a dash for the Doggy Doorway.

Ai Ai! Yeti! Yeti!

Ruff clattered into the kitchen and skidded to a stop on the smooth lino floor, his chest heaving in and out.

Tumble, who had been slumped in her Day Bed, jerked her head up. When she saw Ruff looming in front of her, with streaks of white ꜱɴᴏᴡ in his black fur, she couldn't help but snigger.

"You look like a demented badger!"

Ruff frowned and shook himself vigorously. All the ꜱɴᴏᴡ caught in his fur sprayed out across the kitchen, leaving behind a very shaggy black Scottie dog. And a very wet kitchen.

"Ok. Now you look more like yourself: a demented Scottie!" smirked Tumble.

"This is no time for joking around Tumble! There's a Yeti next door! It's right up against the fence to the Pack Lands!" growled Ruff.

Tumble scowled. She was about to tell Ruff off for talking to her in such a rude way - *I am a*

Royal Princess! – but she had an uncomfortable feeling that he might be right.

I'd almost forgotten about the Yetis. And I can't ignore them as Ruff imagination, like I did the Goblins. I've seen them myself! Lots of them, all over the Moors!

"Right!" she said. "What we need is a plan! A plan to stop the Yeti getting into the Pack Lands."

Ruff skittered about on the floor in excitement, eager that Tumble seemed to be taking the Invasion of the Dog Eating Yetis seriously at last. "But there's more than one Yeti," he pointed out. "Remember, there's another one, two Pack Lands away."

"A plan to keep both of the Yetis out of the Pack Lands," amended Tumble.

"For all we know there might be a whole host of them waiting to bash down the Garden Gate!" said Ruff, glancing nervously in the direction of the Doggy Doorway.

"A plan to make sure NO Yetis get into the Pack Lands."

Ruff sat down and scratched behind his ear. "Mmmm? Perhaps you could herd..."

"A plan that doesn't involve any herding!" growled Tumble. "Or any tree stumps!"

Ruff frowned. "Will this plan involve any help from you?" he asked.

"What is that supposed to mean?" snapped Tumble.

"Well, you normally just laze around in your

bed whilst I have to do all the work."

"How dare you! I do not laze around, I...," began Tumble.

"Laser round! Laser round!" shouted Ruff, his eyes wide and bright.

"Look!" snarled Tumble. "I have just..."

"No, no. Not laze around: laser round. Like, I could blast it with a round from my laser!"

"What laser?" asked Tumble, looking very puzzled. "And what is a round?"

But Ruff had dived into his bed and was busy scuffing up the fleecy mattress. He tossed a number of things aside; a fir cone, a well chewed piece of driftwood, a stub of Chewie, a pencil with a wobbly thing on the end and the remains of what had once been a tennis ball. Eventually he surfaced with a short, metallic cylinder in his mouth.

"Ish asher!" he mumbled triumphantly around his mouthful.

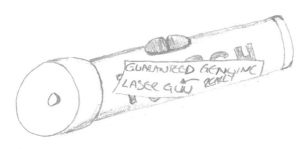

Tumble frowned and raised an eyebrow.

Ruff spat the cylinder onto his fleecy mattress. "This laser!" he repeated.

"That is a torch," stated Tumble.

"No! It might look like a torch. But it is a laser gun. It will zap the Yeti with a round, or shot, of white hot light, melting its EVIL heart!"

"Ruff, it is a torch."

"No!" insisted Ruff. "I bought it on the internet from a **TOP SECRET** spy store that has all the latest secret gadgets. It's a laser gun. Used by all the world's top spies. Look, it even says so on the side," said Ruff pointing at the laser gun with his paw.

Tumble looked at the paper label stating, "GUARANTEED GENUINE LASER GUN – REALLY," that had been poorly stuck to the side of the torch. "How did you find this 'top secret spy store' you bought this torc...laser gun from?" she queried.

"I did an internet search," replied Ruff.

"And you think it's a *real* top secret spy store? With *real* spy gadgets?"

"Of course. It came top of the search so it must be the *most* real top secret spy store!"

"Mmmm?" Tumble wasn't so sure. *I don't think a 'top secret' spy store would be found so easily.* "It doesn't sound very top secret, Ruff!"

"**WELL IT IS!**" snapped Ruff. "**SO THERE!**" Sticking his tongue out at Tumble, Ruff snatched up his laser gun and barged his way out through the Doggy Doorway.

Ruff huffed over to the shrubs and pushed his way through to the fence, muttering about Tumble the whole way.

Humph! Stupid Tumble! She's never any help! Always leaves everything to me. Just because she thinks she's a stupid Princess. And that I'm a servant!

He glanced between the fence slats. *Stupid Yeti's still there! Well he'll wish he'd never thought of eating us once his stupid head is blown off! That will teach him a stupid lesson!*

Ruff fumbled with the laser gun, trying to switch it on. He was concentrating very hard, making sure it wasn't pointing at him. *I don't want to teach myself a lesson!*

"So, what can I do then?" blurted Tumble in his ear.

"ARGGH!" screamed Ruff, dropping the laser gun in the snow.

"Shhh!" warned Tumble.

"Keep the noise down; there's a Yeti just there."

"I know that! What are you doing here," hissed Ruff.

"I thought you wanted some help," growled Tumble.

"Well, creeping up and shouting in my ear isn't much help. I could have blasted my head off with my lethal laser gun!" complained Ruff, scowling at the hole in the snow through which the laser gun had disappeared.

"Mmmm," mumbled Tumble.

"Look, back up under the shrubs and we'll make a plan," suggested Ruff.

Ruff quickly dug the laser gun out of the snow and shoved it in his Back Pocket before joining Tumble under the shrubs. He peered through the leaves to make sure the Yeti couldn't see them. Satisfied he turned to Tumble.

"Right. In my dream last night, *Righteous Rufus* defeated the Yetis in the FANTASY REALM and I was hoping that would mean that the Yetis here would have disappeared too. But they haven't. So now it's down to us to stop their invasion."

"How are we going to do that?" asked Tumble.

"I don't know," admitted Ruff. "I was going to start by blasting this one's head off," he continued, pointing his nose in the direction of the Yeti next door.

"With your laser gun?"

"**YES**," snarled Ruff, giving Tumble a very ferocious **Look**. *You'd better not make any nasty comments about my fantastic laser gun.*

"Well, it would be a start, but there were hundreds of Yetis on the Moors. How did *Righteous Rufus* defeat them?" queried Tumble, wondering why Ruff was squinting at her.

When he was sure Tumble wasn't going to

say anything horrible, Ruff stopped glaring at her. Instead, he turned his gaze up, through the leaves of the shrubs, at the cloud enshrouded sky. There wasn't a chink of blue sky or sunlight to be seen.

"*Righteous Rufus* went on a mission to bring back the sun," said Ruff. "That's how he defeated the Yetis in the FANTASY REALM."

"Bring the sun back!?" exclaimed Tumble. "Wouldn't it have been a bit heavy? And hot?"

"He didn't actually carry it back," said Ruff, returning his gaze to Tumble. "He travelled through the jungle to the Lost City of the Stinkas and…"

"Stinkas?" interrupted Tumble.

"A lost civilisation. The Stinkas are a tribe of miniature, pot bellied pigs."

"Pot bellied pigs? What use would they be?"

"They worship Stinki – the God of the Sun!" declared Ruff.

"So?"

"So, they were holding a Squealer Tournament and…"

"What is a wheeler ornament?"

"No, a Squealer Tournament," corrected Ruff.

"Oh. I'm glad you sorted that out. That makes much more sense!"

"Look, if you would just keep quiet for two minutes and let me finish I will explain!" snarled Ruff.

"Ok! Don't get your tail in a tangle!"

"That wasn't just an expression! I would actually like you to be quiet for two minutes!"

Tumble quietly stuck her tongue out.

"A Squealer Tournament is a competition," explained Ruff, ignoring Tumble's rudeness. *At least she's keeping quiet.* "The contestants ride around on squealers." Seeing Tumble frown, Ruff added, "Which are a Stinka version of screelers." The frown deepened. "You know? Like those flat board things with wheels underneath that were on the Flickery Light Box With Noises last night."

"Oh! You mean skateboards."

Skateboards! Of course! Roller skate, scrubbing board: skateboard! Brilliant!!

"Yeh! Like skateboards. Anyway. The contestants had to ride the squealers around a course, doing jumps and tricks over pyramids and ramps and rails. *Righteous Rufus* used a Top Secret Gadget Board and won the tournament with a spectacular final jump using the built in jet boosters."

"So, he cheated."

"No! There wasn't anything in the rules about

not using a jet booster! Anyway, the Stinkas were very primitive and didn't know what a jet booster was. They thought he had god-like powers."

"So, how did all this help him bring back the sun?"

"Ah! The prize for winning the tournament was a magical disc of solid gold that carried the power of the Sun God, Stinki. *Righteous Rufus* raced back to the ꜰꜰᴀɴᴛᴀꜱʏ ʀᴇᴀʟᴍ in his Turbo Powered Pop-Up Pocket Paraglider. When he got there he placed the ɢᴏʟᴅᴇɴ ᴅɪꜱᴄ ᴏꜰ ᴛʜᴇ ꜱᴜɴ ɢᴏᴅ ꜱᴛɪɴᴋɪ on top of the highest tower of the Palace. The sun broke through the clouds, melting all the ꜱɴᴏᴡ and ɪᴄᴇ. The

Yetis were defeated and had to retreat into the depths of the mountains."

"Of course. So, let me guess: your plan is to go to the Lost City of the Stinka, play squeaker games and bring the sun back," mocked Tumble with a smirk on her face.

"Don't be stupid, Tumble. We don't know how to get past the Garden Gate. So, unless the Lost City is somewhere in the garden, we can't. Otherwise it would be a good plan. But maybe we could make a sun!"

"Make a sun? How are we going to make a sun? The sun is a vast ball of hotness that hangs in the sky!"

"It's not vast," protested Ruff. "It's not even as big as my old rubber ball. Ooooo! Perhaps we could paint that yellow and hang it from a tree!"

"Ruff, the sun only looks smaller than your

 manky old rubber ball because it is a long way away. It is vast!"

"How vast? And how far away?"

"Er...," erred Tumble, looking around the garden, trying to think of something really big. "Ah! It is bigger than the house! And...er...and even higher up than the clouds. And most of the time, when it's not foggy, those are even higher up than the trees."

Ruff frowned. "Oh. Ok then, we won't make a sun." He sat down and scratched behind his ear trying to get his Third Brain Cell working. "Ooooo! If we can't make a sun, perhaps we can find something else that makes a lot of heat to melt all the snow."

"Like what?" asked Tumble.

"Mmmm? Well, there are some things in the kitchen that might work. There are matches in the drawer. We could make a fire."

"That sounds a bit dangerous," said Tumble

"Not as dangerous as an Invasion of Dog

Eating Yetis," objected Ruff.

"Still sounds a bit risky," insisted Tumble.

"Ok," grumbled Ruff. "Oooo, what about chillies, they're really hot."

"Don't be daft, Ruff. How can chilly be hot. Chilly means cold."

"Not chilly – chilli," said Ruff.

"Of course, silly me. That's very clear."

Ruff wasn't sure if Tumble really meant that or if she was just being sarcastic. To make sure he explained, "Chillies are small pointy vegetables that are really, really hot if you eat them." Ruff knew this because the Pack Leader had dropped one when he was cooking and Ruff had gobbled it up before the Pack Leader could stop him. *I had to drain my water bowl three times before the fire in my tummy went out!* "There are probably some in the

131

Big White Keep Things COLD Cupboard."

Tumble thought about it. "That's a good plan. But only if we can make the Yetis eat them."

"Mmmm?" Ruff scratched again. "I know! We could drag the Really Hot Cupboard That Burns Food (And Noses if You Sniff to Close) into the garden. If we open the door it will blast out enough heat to melt all the snow and ICE in the world. It's hotter than the sun!" growled Ruff with feeling: he had sniffed too close.

They were interrupted by the sound of shouting children coming from next door.

"Oh no! The children from the Pack Lands next door will be eaten alive! We have to defeat the Yeti before it gets them!" shouted Ruff.

"Right!" barked Tumble, suddenly all action. "You go and zap the Yeti with your torc...laser gun and I'll go and get the Really Hot Cupboard That Burns Food (And Noses if You Sniff to Close)." She turned and scuttled across the garden in a flurry of kicked up snow before disappearing through the Doggy Doorway with a clatter clunk.

Ruff pushed his way through the shrubs to the fence once more. Glancing between the slats he could see the children hurling snowballs at each other.

"LOOK OUT!" warned Ruff. "Yeti!"

The children must have heard and understood because they instantly turned in Ruff's direction and started hurling snow-balls at the Yeti. Unfortunately their aim was not very good and most of the snowballs smashed into the fence in front of him, scattering snow all over his fur again.

The Yeti didn't take much notice of any of this. *Perhaps it's asleep. I'll blast it whilst it isn't looking!*

Whilst Ruff fumbled his laser gun out of his Back Pocket the children gave up hurling snowballs at the stupid barking dog next door and started booting a football around in the snow.

Ruff, meanwhile, pointed his laser gun at the Yeti's head. Trembling with nerves and excitement, he clicked the switch. The laser gun flashed a lethal beam of light straight at the Yeti's head!

This lit it up nicely but didn't blast it into powder snow.

Blast! Or not blast.

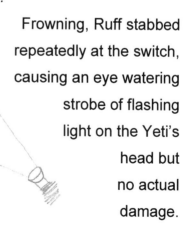

Frowning, Ruff stabbed repeatedly at the switch, causing an eye watering strobe of flashing light on the Yeti's head but no actual damage.

Scowling, Ruff looked more closely at the laser gun's controls. *Ah! If I slide this bit forward it will make the laser beam much more narrow and deadly. Strong enough to blast the* Yeti's *head off.*

Ruff pointed the laser gun at the Yeti's head again. He backed up slightly to get a better aim, accidentally nudging the shrub behind him. As he clicked the switch to zap the Yeti, a clump of snow dropped from the shrub into his eyes.

At that very moment, one of the children next door made a wild kick at the football. It flew straight and true, smacking into the Yeti's head, knocking it from its shoulders. But Ruff didn't see this because he was panicking.

Arrrrgh! I can't see. I can't see! The Yeti

has used it powers to blind me with **ICE**. He shook himself vigorously, the **snow** flying in sprays from his eyes.

Ha! I can see again! And look!! I've blasted the Yeti's *head off! It's dead. I killed it!*

Just then there was a gust of wind and the colourful ninja star in the Yeti's hand started spinning.

Poopscoops! *It's still alive!*

Ruff scuttled through the shrubs, across the garden and clattered into the kitchen through the Doggy Doorway.

There he found Tumble curled up in her Day Bed as if nothing was happening. Ruff scowled and gave her a **GLARE** – which is like a **Look** but much worse.

"I thought **you** were getting the Really Hot Cupboard That Burns Food (And Noses if You Sniff to Close)," growled Ruff.

"Oh! Was I? Yes! Well...er..." mumbled Tumble, trying to think of an excuse. She had come in to the kitchen with every intention of

getting the Really Hot Cupboard That Burns Food (And Noses if You Sniff to Close). But once she was away from Ruff's constant babble about the Yetis she had started to have doubts.

*After all, the Yetis on the Moors weren't **very** deadly. I defeated one easily by knocking its head off. And then it disappeared leaving only a couple of giant snowballs!*

Something wasn't quite right with that but she wasn't sure what. *Does it mean that they aren't even real?*

So, she had got into her nice warm, cosy bed to think about it. And fallen asleep.

"Well er...what?" demanded Ruff

"Well er...I tried but the Really Hot Cupboard That Burns Food (And Noses if You Sniff to Close) is far too heavy for me to move on my own. So I climbed into bed to have a think." Tumble smiled to herself, very pleased with her excuse. *And it's all true.*

"And **what** did you think?"

Oh! That's awkward. "Er...I thought it was really warm and cosy," Tumble grinned. When she saw Ruff frowning her grin flattened out. "Er...and then I thought..." or at least now she thought, "...if the Yetis don't like heat, then maybe they won't bother me in my bed. Because it's warm."

Ruff's frown deepened to a scowl.

I can't believe it. I'm out there in the icy cold, risking my life, fighting vicious, ninja, Dog Eating Yetis and Tumble's in here, warm and cosy in her bed!

Ruff growled in frustration.

Why didn't I think of that!

He padded over to his bed, curled up and settled down for a quick Forty Winks.

Chapter Nine

Visit of the Sun God

Ruff couldn't settle into his Forty Winks. It was nagging at the back of his mind that he couldn't really stop the Invasion of the Dog Eating Yetis by sitting in bed.

A gust of icy wind pushed the Doggy Doorway open, letting in a swirl of snow and the screams of the children next door.

The children next door! Ruff leapt to his paws, growling deep in his chest. *I'd forgotten about them! The Yeti must be attacking them. Now I've blasted its head off it's probably just randomly chucking ninja throwing stars around! I've got to try and save them!*

Leaving the safe heat of his Day Bed, Ruff rushed outside. There was a lot of shouting coming from the next door garden. *They're dying! Or at least writhing in agony!*

Ruff charged across the garden, smashed through the shrubs, skidded in the ﬓﬔﬗ and thudded into the fence. He scrambled back to his paws and peered through a gap.

The Yeti's still holding its ninja throwing star so it isn't attacking.

Poopscoops! *Its head has grown back!*

Something bright caught his eye. The children were shouting and throwing some bright yellow thing at each other.

They should be throwing it at the Yeti, not each other!

"HEY KIDS!" barked Ruff. "THROW IT AT THE Yeti! THROW IT AT THE Yeti!"

The next moment the thing came hurtling towards him. Luckily the fence was in the way. Ruff backed through the shrubs out of range.

Those kids are useless shots! How could they miss that massive great Yeti? And how did it get its head back on? It looks like blasting Yetis with a laser gun isn't going to work.

Tumble appeared through the Doggy Doorway and tramped through the 𝕤𝕟𝕠𝕨.

"What's all the ruckus?" she complained. "I was trying to sleep."

"How can you be sleeping when there's an Invasion of Dog Eating Yetis going on?"

"Er...well it was very warm and..." Tumble trailed off feeling a bit guilty that she wasn't helping with the Yeti's. But she still wasn't sure if they were quite real. *And even if they are, they don't seem much of a threat.* "Ruff, are you sure the Yetis are real."

"Of course they are real! There's one just over the fence. And another one, two Pack Lands away. Look, if you do this," said Ruff, balancing on his hind legs and hopping up to get the height he needed to see over the shrubs and through a gap in the fence, "you can see its

scarf flapping in the breeze."

Tumble, who felt it beneath her to act like a circus dog, took his word for it.

"Yes, but they're not very active are they."

"What do you mean?" asked Ruff suspiciously.

"They don't move a lot. They're not very threatening."

"Well of course *these* Yetis aren't moving much. They're spies. They're just here to keep an eye on us."

"They're not moving *at all*," insisted Tumble.

"They are! The one next door keeps threatening me by spinning a ninja throwing star in his hand." When Tumble didn't look overly impressed he added, "And when I blasted its head off with my laser gun it grew back!"

"Really?"

"Yes!"

Tumble was a little worried now. *Something that can grow a new head might be a bit of a threat.*

She remembered the Yeti on the Moors.

I knocked its head off and it turned into two giant snowballs. Or did it? Perhaps it just looked like that. Perhaps when we had gone, it grew another head. Perhaps it's searching for me, right now, looking for revenge!

"We're going to have to try and drag the Really Hot Cupboard That Burns Food (And Noses if You Sniff to Close) into the garden and melt it," declared Ruff.

"What good will melting it do?" asked Tumble with a frown.

"Well, I'm pretty sure even a Yeti won't be able to recover from being melted!"

"Oh, the Yeti! I thought you wanted to melt the Really Hot Cupboard That Burns Food (And Noses if You Sniff to Close)."

"That," said Ruff, "would be stupid. Come on, let's go and get it."

"Er...which 'it' are we talking about now? The Yeti or the Really Hot Cupboard That Burns Food (And Noses if You Sniff to Close)?" asked Tumble, starting to get confused.

"The Really Hot Cupboard That Burns Food (And Noses if You Sniff to Close) of course," growled Ruff.

"We can't. It won't fit through the Doggy Doorway," said Tumble, who had done at least a little bit of thinking about the problem, whilst curled up in her warm and cosy bed.

"Oh yeh," sighed Ruff, his shoulders slumping. He scratched behind his ear, desperately trying to think. "Oooo! Perhaps we could persuade the Yeti to climb inside the

Really Hot Cupboard That Burns Food (And Noses if You Sniff to Close) and then slam the door on it."

"Don't be daft, Ruff. How are we ever going to do that?"

"Well, Hansel and Gretel managed it with that witch," pointed out Ruff.

"Mmmm, it's a good point," conceded Tumble. "But I'm not sure how true that story is. You know how long we've been hunting for the gingerbread house in the **Woods** and we've never even found a crumb. I think it's an EVIL story told to disappoint poor HUNGRY dogs. And even if we could persuade the Yeti, he's too big for the Doggy Doorway anyway."

Ruff humphed and then scratched some more. "I know! We'll build a fire and melt it into a puddle!"

145

"I've already said, a fire would be too dangerous, Ruff."

"It's the only way!" insisted Ruff. "If we don't do something soon, all those Yeti's from the Moors will be knocking down the Garden Gate. In fact they might be coming up the street right now!"

"Do you think so?" asked Tumble, her wide eyes darting in the direction of the Garden Gate. In all the chat about gingerbread houses she had forgotten about the ravening, Dog Eating Yeti from the Moors that was out for her blood.

"I'm sure! They've had plenty of time to get here!"

"That's true," mumbled Tumble, looking a little quivery around the knees. Her mind was alive with the image of a rabid, killer, possibly headless, Dog Eating Yeti smashing down the gate and chomping her up in revenge.

ARRRGGH!

"WHAT?! WHAT?!" yelp Tumble, leaping into the air in fright.

"I heard a Yeti at the Garden Gate!!"

"I didn't hear any..."

"Quick! Grab things to burn. I'll get the matches!" barked Ruff over his shoulder as he charged towards the Doggy Doorway.

"What things to burn!?" asked Tumble, a tremble of panic in her voice. But Ruff had already disappeared into the kitchen.

Tumble searched around the garden, desperately trying to find things that would burn. *Everything is buried under the snow! I need wood. Ah! Shrubs! They're made of wood. And leaves. Leaves burn!*

In a frenzy, Tumble began to tear shrubs out of the frozen earth. As she piled them up in a heap, in the middle of the garden, there was a tremendous crash from the kitchen. A few moments later Ruff clattered through the Doggy Doorway with the matches in his mouth.

"Quick, quick! Light the bonfire," shouted Tumble.

For the next few minutes the only sounds were the shouts of the children next door and the scratch and scrape of matches being dragged across a matchbox and failing to burst into FLAMES.

"Hurry up, Ruff!"

"Gis ishn't easy goo know!" **grumbled** Ruff around a mouthful of matches as he tried to strike them against the box he held between his paws.

But it was pointless. Ruff had **DRIBBLED** all over the matches and they were useless. He spat them out in disgust.

"Blast! We've had it now," he moaned.

"We're doomed!"

At that very moment, a bright yellow disc flew over the fence and landed at Ruff's paws.

For a second or two he looked at it in shock. Then his eyes widened. "ᵀᴴᴱ ᴳᴼᴸᴰᴱᴺ ᴰᴵˢᶜ ᴼᶠ ᵀᴴᴱ ˢᵁᴺ ᴳᴼᴰ ˢᵀᴵᴺᴷᴵ! Tumble, it's the golden disc that *Righteous Rufus* won at the Squealer Tournament!"

"Is it? It looks like a flying disc to me."

"No! It is a magical golden disc, with the power of the Sun God, Stinki!"

Tumble frowned. It definitely looked like a flying disc to her, the sort she had seen children throwing to each other in the park.

Ruff picked up the ᴳᴼᴸᴰᴱᴺ ᴰᴵˢᶜ ᴼᶠ ᵀᴴᴱ ˢᵁᴺ ᴳᴼᴰ ˢᵀᴵᴺᴷᴵ gently between his teeth. He clambered up the side of the bonfire and wedged it between the branches of the topmost shrub, the highest point in the garden he could reach.

He scrambled back down and sat next to Tumble. Shoulder to shoulder they watched the disc in awe and waited.

Actually, Ruff watched the disc in awe; Tumble watched it in doubt. But they both waited.

And then...

nothing happened.

"Ruff, it's just a flying disc," suggested Tumble quietly.

"Shhh!" hissed Ruff.

In the silence that followed something finally happened: Tumble realised that if the GOLDEN DISC OF THE SUN GOD STINKI was a load of old rubbish then it was probably true that the whole Dog Eating Yeti thing was also nonsense. Ruff had fooled her into believing his daft stories again.

And this time, instead of herding a tree stump he's made me rip up the Pack Leader's shrubs and build a massive bonfire in the middle of the garden!

Tumble was about to explode in a rage when a dazzling ray of sunlight stabbed down from the sky, lighting the yellow disc with a golden radiance.

Frowning, Tumble turned her gaze upward. The clouds were breaking apart revealing blue sky. The heat of the sun beamed down on her face.

"And so the Invasion of the Dog Eating Yetis is defeated," said Ruff in a serious voice.

HOORAY!!!

Ruff gave a bark of joy and then, job done, he trotted into the house for a well earned Forty Winks.

Speechless, Tumble watched Ruff disappear through the Doggy Doorway and then turned to stare at the GOLDEN DISC OF THE SUN GOD STINKI.

It still looks like a flying disc to me.

But the 𝕤𝕟𝕠𝕨 on the shed roof was already melting, drops of water tumbling from the eaves to drive little holes into the 𝕤𝕟𝕠𝕨 on the ground below. *It does seem to have the power of the Sun God Stinki though.*

So we have done it then. We have defeated the Invasion of the Dog Eating Yeti.

Tumble sat in silence for a while enjoying the heat of the sun on her back.

Did we really? Were they real?

There was a soft ploof as thawing 𝕤𝕟𝕠𝕨 dropping from the branches of the shrubs. The surviving shrubs.

Tumble looked at the pile of ripped up shrubs in the middle of the garden and grimaced.

One thing that is for real: the Pack Leader is NOT going to be happy when he sees that!

The End

OTHER BOOKS

To find out more about their first adventure, Invasion of the Goblin Horde, join Ruff and Tumble on facebook:

www.facebook.com/ruffand tumble1.

To find out more about other books written by Royston Wood visit:
www.books-4-children.com

Or for the latest news see his latest blog here -
http://roystonwood.blogspot.co.uk/

ABOUT THE AUTHOR

As a child I was not a keen reader. I didn't see the point: there were comics and a picture is worth a thousand words, right?

Now I am an avid reader and regret missing out on so many good stories as a kid. Fortunately, with children of my own, I'm now managing to catch up, reading stories to them every night before bed.

There isn't anything quite like a book to let you escape from real life for a while. True, films are great, but they don't involve you as much as a book. A well written book will get your imagination working, filling the story with colour and energy, making the story yours. A film is just a depiction of somebody else's imagination.

In fact, I enjoy reading stories to my children so much, I started to write my own. And bearing in mind my own reluctance to read as a child I have written them to be as engaging as possible, to draw the reader into a land of imagination and discovery.